on a great book
this summer!

Happy Reading! Summer 2022

P9-DTA-450

I blame Jory.
—J.C.

It's not my fault.
—J.J.

Text copyright © 2020 by Jory John
Jacket art and interior illustrations copyright © 2020 by Jared Chapman

All rights reserved. Published in the United States by Random House Children's Books,
a division of Penguin Random House LLC, New York.

Random House and the colophon are registered trademarks of Penguin Random House LLC.

Visit us on the Web! rhcbooks.com

Educators and librarians, for a variety of teaching tools, visit us at RHTeachersLibrarians.com

Library of Congress Cataloging-in-Publication Data is available upon request.
ISBN 978-1-9848-3060-9 (trade) — ISBN 978-1-9848-3061-6 (lib. bdg.) —
ISBN 978-1-9848-3062-3 (ebook)

Book design by Nicole de las Heras

MANUFACTURED IN CHINA
10 9 8 7 6 5 4 3 2 1
First Edition

IT'S NOT MY FAULT!

words by
Jory John

art by
Jared Chapman

Random House ⌂ New York

Why is your homework so messy?
It's not *my* fault! I blame my pen.

Why can't I read these test answers?
I blame my pen.

Why is your assignment so late?
Um . . . I blame my pen?

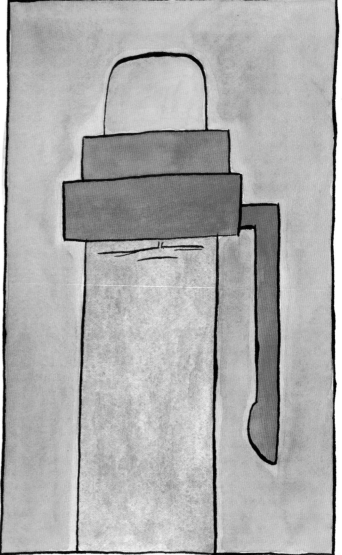

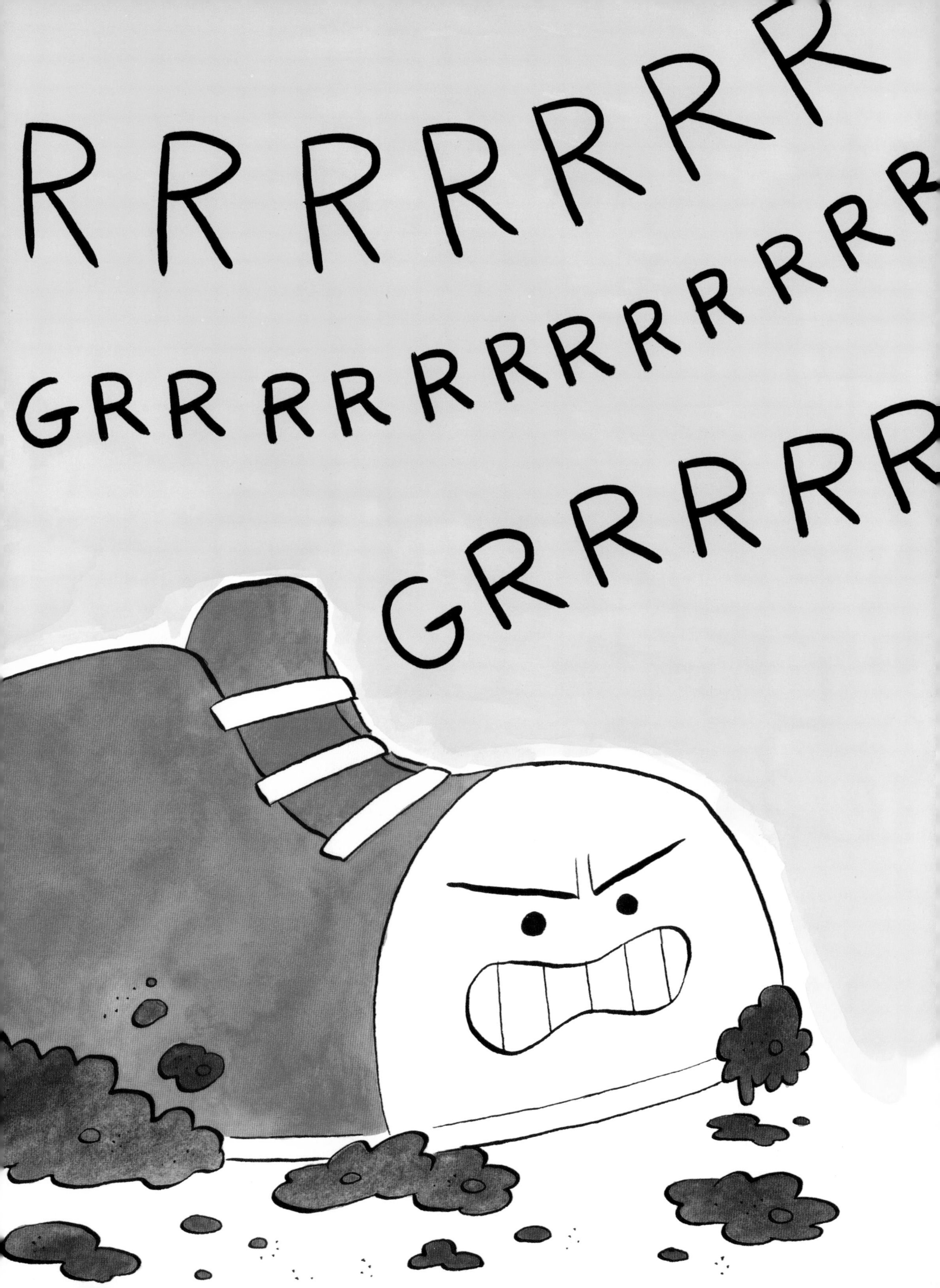
RRRRRRR
GRRRRRRRRRRRR
GRRRRRR

Messy hair? I blame my comb.
Muddy face? I blame my soap.
Gunk in teeth? I blame my toothbrush.

Missing homework? I blame my backpack.

Unmade bed? I blame my pillows. And my sheets.
And my comforter.

Why are you up so late?
I blame the moon.

GRRRRRR

Hello. It is *I*, your trusty pen. I am here with an important message. Listen: I know you think you've figured out how life works. But let me tell you this: You surely haven't. Here's the thing: Blaming everything but yourself, never taking responsibility for your actions, and pointing a guilty, quaking finger whenever you've done anything wrong is a *sham*. Deep in your heart, you *know* this. Did your humble shoes really deserve all the blame for the mud, for the leaves, for the footprints on the wall?

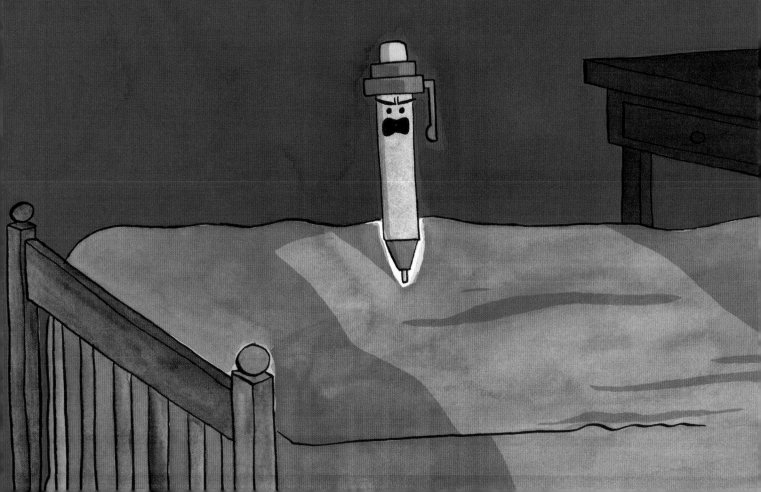

And I ask you: Did your poor backpack deserve 100 percent of the blame for losing homework you should've been more careful with? Huh? Was it really the backpack's fault?

Calm down, dear Backpack. I've got this. Listen to me now, kid: Your bed was messy, not because of the covers, not because of the pillows, but because you refused to make it, even though it takes less than two minutes. Okay? Your face was muddy because you played in a puddle. Not because of any deficiency in your soap products. You had gunk in your teeth because you insist on eating junk. And then you don't floss afterward. There's only so much a toothbrush can do. And blaming the moon for when you stay up too late makes literally NO SENSE AT ALL. You know this.

So I will simply add: If you continue to blame everything around you for all the things you do, we won't want to be your friend anymore. We won't want to spend time with you. And that thought breaks my heart because I know you're a mostly good kid with mostly good intentions.

Wait! No. I *don't* blame my pen. . . .

At least, not totally. After all, I held the pen. I controlled the pen. I'd say we share the blame, 70/30 ... maybe 80/20. I mostly blame ... *me.*

Wow. Well ... that's not what I expected to hear from you.

And while I'm at it, I no longer blame my shoes,
my backpack, my comb, my pillows, my sheets,
my comforter, my soap, my toothbrush, and the moon.
These are all simply inanimate objects—at least,
most of the time—who took the blame while I got
away with everything. I'd like to take this moment
to apologize to them, too.

I am tired of blaming literally everything and everyone except myself. I will try to do better ... starting now! With that said, I will get back to work on this math. . . .

Whoops ... um ... ink.

Oh no ... *ink!*
Sheesh ...
SO MUCH INK!

Go ahead. Do it. Blame your pen. This would be the perfect opportunity.

I . . . I . . . can't. I can't do it. I probably didn't take good-enough care of the pen. I blame . . . *myself.* Sigh.

Well, I'm impressed. Now please clean up all this ink. It's everywhere.

Psst! Hey! Pen! Were you testing me? It seemed like a test. Did I pass? You have to admit, that one *was* sort of your fault, Pen.

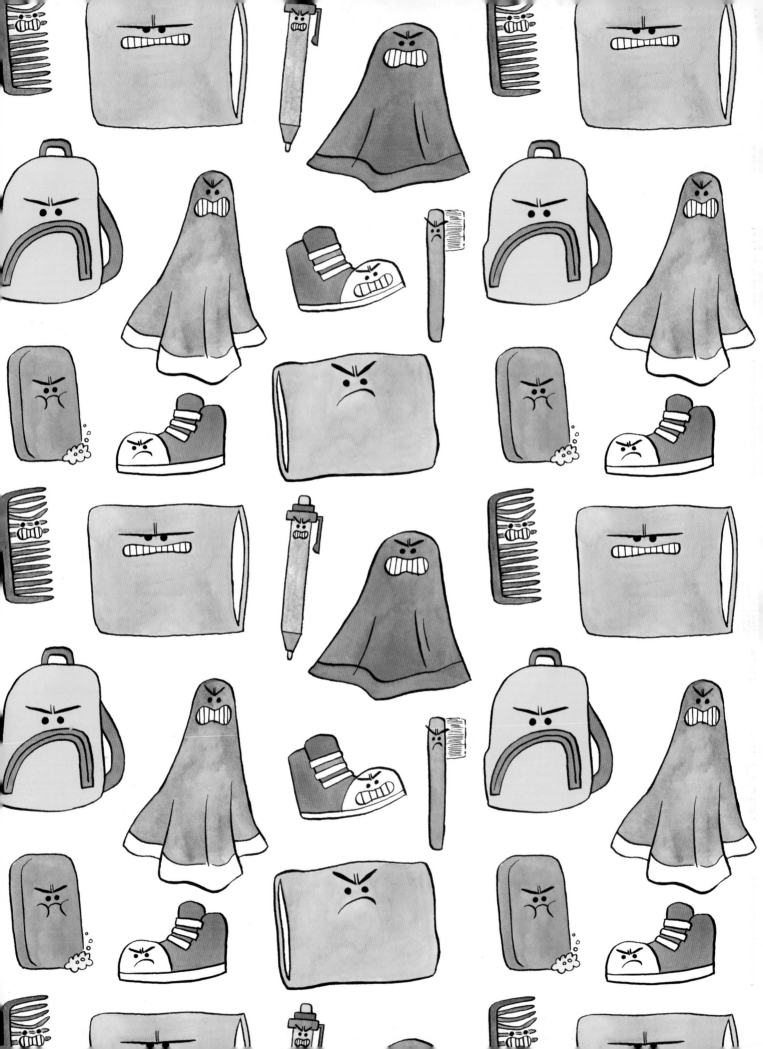